THE BEAR
DETECTIVES

For Joshua Ainley
– I know your grandma and grandpa!
S.G.

For Jake
J.B.

ORCHARD BOOKS
338 Euston Road, London NW1 3BH
*Orchard Books Australia*
Hachette Children's Books
Level 17/207 Kent Street, Sydney NSW 2000

First published in 2009
First paperback publication in 2010

Text © Sally Grindley 2009
Illustrations © Jo Brown 2009

The rights of Sally Grindley to be identified as the author and
Jo Brown to be identified as the illustrator of this work
have been asserted by them in accordance with the
Copyright, Designs and Patents Act, 1988.

A CIP catalogue record for this book is available from the British Library

ISBN 978 1 84616 154 4 (hardback)
ISBN 978 1 84616 162 9 (paperback)

1 3 5 7 9 10 8 6 4 2 (hardback)
1 3 5 7 9 10 8 6 4 2 (paperback)

Printed in China

Orchard Books is a division of Hachette Children's Books,
an Hachette UK company.

www.hachette.co.uk

# A Very Important Day

Written by **SALLY GRINDLEY**
Illustrated by **JO BROWN**

ORCHARD BOOKS

Constable Tiggs

Sergeant Bumble

Alvin Crackem

Sergeant Bumble and Constable
Tiggs began work early one
morning.

"Today is an important day," said
Bumble.
"Yes," said Tiggs. "Very important."

"Just think, Alvin Crackem, the greatest pawballer in the world, will soon be here to open our new stadium," said Bumble.
"I'm excited!" said Tiggs.
"I can't wait to meet him."

"A police constable on duty has no time to be excited," said Bumble. He opened a cupboard. "I'd better try out the match ball, just to make sure it's all right."

"Be careful, Sir," said Tiggs.
"I'll show you how it's done," said
Bumble. He placed the ball on the
ground and kicked it. "Catch!"

The ball flew past Tiggs's hands
and straight through the window.
"Oh no!" cried Tiggs.
"You were supposed to catch it,"
grumbled Bumble.

They ran to the window, just in time to see the ball land in a passing truck.

"Stop!" cried Tiggs.

"Chase that truck!" cried Bumble.

"We must have the ball back
before the Grand Opening."

They jumped into
the police car...

...and raced after
the truck, with the
blue light flashing.

At last, the truck stopped. Tiggs
jumped into the back of it.
"Catch, Sergeant Bumble!" he
called.

Bumble clapped his hands together and missed. "A terrible throw, Constable Tiggs," he grumbled.

The ball bounced onto the road.
Just then, a dog ran up, grabbed it,
and ran off across the green.
"Stop that dog!" yelled Bumble.

They raced after
the dog as fast
as they could.

But before they could
catch up, he reached
the village pond
and jumped in.
"Oh no!"
cried Tiggs.

The dog swam to the other side
of the pond and let go of the ball.
Then he jumped out, wagged his
tail and ran off.

"I'll have you arrested!" Bumble
called after him.

Tiggs ran round the pond.
Bumble panted after him.
They were almost there when
they saw a small bear wade
into the water and pick up
the ball.

"Stop!" cried Bumble.
The bear didn't hear him. He got
on his bike and rode away, with
the ball tucked under his arm.
"Oh no!" cried Tiggs.

"I need to catch my breath," puffed Bumble. He sat down at the roadside.

"What are we going to do?" asked Tiggs. "It's nearly time for the Grand Opening."

The sound of a horn made them both jump. The biggest car they had ever seen stopped right by them, and a window opened.

"Can I offer you a lift?" came a voice from inside. Tiggs bent down to whisper in Bumble's ear. "It's him! It's Alvin Crackem!" he exclaimed.

"Welcome to our v-village,
Mr Crackem, Sir. We were just
on our w-way to the Grand
Opening," spluttered Bumble.
"Then we can all go together,"
said Alvin Crackem.

They climbed into the car.
"I say!" said Bumble, when
he felt the soft seats.
"Wow!" said Tiggs, when
he saw the television.

"So it's your job to solve problems
in the village, is it?" asked Alvin.
"It's a very important job," said
Bumble. "And right now we have
a big problem to solve."

"We've lost the match ball," said
Tiggs sadly.
"Well, I can solve that problem for
you!" said Alvin.

He pulled out a brand-new ball
from under his seat. "We'll use this
one instead," he said.

"How kind of you, Mr Crackem,
Sir!" exclaimed Bumble.

"Look, we're here!" cried Tiggs.

Bumble and Tiggs
showed Alvin Crackem
into the stadium.

"The fans are all waiting to welcome you!" said Bumble. The crowds cheered and cheered as Alvin Crackem waved at them.

Bumble threw the match ball
to the waiting teams.
"Would you do us the
honour, Mr Crackem, Sir,
of declaring our brand-new
stadium open?" he said.

Alvin Crackem went to the
middle of the pitch. "I now
declare your brand-new
stadium open!" he said.
"Let the pawball match begin!"

# THE BEAR DETECTIVES

## SALLY GRINDLEY & JO BROWN

| | |
|---|---|
| Bucket Rescue | 978 1 84616 160 5 |
| Who Shouted Boo? | 978 1 84616 159 9 |
| The Ghost Train | 978 1 84616 161 2 |
| Treasure Hunt | 978 1 84616 158 2 |
| The Mysterious Earth | 978 1 84616 163 6 |
| The Strange Pawprint | 978 1 84616 164 3 |
| The Missing Spaghetti | 978 1 84616 165 0 |
| A Very Important Day | 978 1 84616 162 9 |

All priced at £4.99

Orchard Colour Crunchies are available from all good bookshops,
or can be ordered direct from the publisher:
Orchard Books, PO BOX 29, Douglas IM99 1BQ
Credit card orders please telephone 01624 836000
or fax 01624 837033 or visit our website: www.orchardbooks.co.uk
or e-mail: bookshop@enterprise.net for details.

To order please quote title, author and ISBN
and your full name and address.
Cheques and postal orders should be made payable to 'Bookpost plc.'
Postage and packing is FREE within the UK
(overseas customers should add £2.00 per book).

Prices and availability are subject to change.